Kenji Miyazawa Picture Book Series-7

Crossing the Snow

Original text by Kenji Miyazawa
Translated by Karen Colligan-Taylor
Pictures by Masao Idou

International Foundation for the Promotion of Languages and Culture
(IFLC)

Crossing the Snow
Kenji Miyazawa Picture Book Series -7

All Rights Reserved
First Published 2000

Special thanks to Miyazawa Kenji Museum and
Miyazawa Kenji Iihatobu Museum
Original Text: Kenji Miyazawa
Translation: © Karen Colligan-Taylor 2000
Book Design: Seiichi Suzuki
Illustration: © Masao Idou 2000
Proofreading: Winston Priest
Published by International Foundation for the Promotion of Languages and Culture (IFLC),
Sunmark Bldg., 1-32-13 Takadanobaba, Shinjuku-ku, Tokyo, 169-8639, Japan
TEL: 81-3-5273-6660 FAX: 81-3-5273-6661
Publisher: Keiichi Kajikawa
Distributed by Sunmark Inc., Sunmark Bldg., 1-32-13 Takadanobaba, Shinjuku-ku, Tokyo, 169-8639, Japan

ISBN4-7631-2317-3 C8390

Contents

Part One: The Fox Pup, Konzaburo
Part Two: The Magic Lantern Show at
          the Elementary School

About the Author
About the Story

Part One:
The Fox Pup, Konzaburo

The snow, which had frozen over completely, was now harder than marble, and even the sky appeared to be made from a sheet of cold, smooth, blue stone.

"*Kanko* goes hard snow, *shinko* goes frozen snow."

The sun blazed a pure white and scattered about it the fragrance of lilies. Then, once again it shone down on the snow, making it glisten and glitter, *giragira*.

The frost-laden trees sparkled, *pikapika*, as if they had been sprinkled with sugar.

"Hard snow, *kanko*, frozen snow, *shinko*."

Shiro and Kanko put on their tiny snow boots made of woven rice straw, and went crunching out into the meadow, *kikku kikku kikku*.

Would there ever again be such a wonderful day? Today they were free to head out in any direction they wished, even into places through which they usually couldn't pass, such as fields of millet or meadows choked with pampas grass. Everything was as flat and even as a single board, and the

entire surface glittered as if it were made of a great many tiny mirrors.

"Hard snow, *kanko*, frozen snow, *shinko*."

The two children approached the forest. A large oak bent over heavily, pulled down by the weight of the splendid, clear icicles hanging from its branches.

Facing the forest, the children called out, "Hard snow, *kanko*, frozen snow, *shinko*. The fox child wants a bride; he wants a bride."

For some time all was still and silent. Just as the children had sucked in their breath, ready to shout again, a white fox pup emerged from the forest, chanting, "Hard snow, *kanko*, frozen snow, *shinko*," as it stomped through the snow, *kishiri kishiri*.

Taken by surprise, Shiro stepped in front of Kanko as if to shield her, planted his feet down firmly, and called back, "Fox *kon kon*, white fox! If you want a bride, I'll get one for you."

Though it was still very small to be putting on airs, the fox gave one of its silver, needle-like whiskers a twirl, and replied, "Shiro goes *shinko*, Kanko goes *kanko*. As for me, I don't really need a bride at all."

Shiro laughed, and took up the chant.

"Fox *kon kon*, little fox child, if you don't want a bride, how about some rice cakes?" Then, shaking its head two or three times, the fox pup replied playfully, "Shiro, *shinko*, Kanko, *kanko*, shall I give you some millet dumplings?"

Kanko thought this exchange was so funny that she sang out from behind Shiro, "Fox *kon kon*, little fox child, aren't fox dumplings just rabbit pellets?"

The fox pup, Konzaburo, laughed and explained, "No, not at all, by no means. Would such fine folk as the two of you be likely to eat the rabbit's brown dumplings? People say we deceive and trick them, but I say we've been falsely charged."

"You mean, then, these tales about foxes tricking people are all a lie?" asked Shiro in surprise.

Konzaburo replied earnestly, "All false, they are. The most terrible of lies. People who say they've been tricked by us are the type who drink too much or are natural cowards. It's pretty interesting, you know. Why, not too long ago, Jinbee-san sat in front of our house all of one moonlit night, reciting a play. We all went out and watched him."

"If it was Jinbee-san, it wasn't a play he was reciting. It was more likely a popular song," shouted Shiro.

This seemed to make sense to Konzaburo, for he added, "That could very well be. At any rate, please have some dumplings. These dumplings I'm offering you are ones for which I myself plowed the fields, sowed the seed, harvested the millet grass, pounded it into flour, kneaded it, steamed it, and covered it with sugar. How about it? I'd like to give you a plateful."

Shiro laughed. "Konzaburo-san. We just ate some rice cakes before we came over here, so we aren't hungry yet. Could you invite us over again sometime?"

The fox pup Konzaburo batted his short legs together happily, *batabata*. "Is that right? Well, I'll offer you some again when we have our magic lantern party. Please do be sure to come to the slide show. It will be on the next moonlit night when the snow has frozen over. The show starts right at eight, so let me give you some tickets now. How many shall I give you?"

"Well, how about five?" suggested Shiro.

"Five? Two are for you and your sister, but who are the other three for?" asked Konzaburo.

When Shiro replied, "My older brothers," Konzaburo asked, "Are your brothers eleven or under?"

"No, the youngest of my older brothers is in the fourth grade, so that would be eight years plus four more, which would make him twelve."

Konzaburo gave his whisker another twirl with a nonchalant air. "Well, then, I'm very sorry but I'm afraid we can't invite your older brothers. You two should come by yourselves. We'll reserve some special seats for you. It'll be really interesting. The title of the first slide is 'One should not drink liquor.' Here we see two fellows from your village, Taemon and Seisaku, nearly blind from drinking so much sake, as they are about to eat some strange-looking bean-jam buns and some buckwheat noodles out here in the meadow. You'll see me in the slide, as well. The title of the second slide is 'Watch out for traps.' This shows our Konbee entangled in a snare out in the meadow. It's a picture. It's not a photograph. The title of the third slide is 'Don't play with fire.' This is a shot of our Konsuke getting his tail burned when he went to your house. I do

hope you'll join us."

The two joyfully nodded in agreement.

The fox curled his lips in a comical way and began stamping his feet *kikku kikku ton ton kikku kikku ton ton*, all the time wagging his tail and shaking his head back and forth. For a while he seemed to be lost in thought, but at last he must have stumbled on an idea, for he suddenly began to sing, marking the beat with his paws.

"Frozen snow, *shinko*, hard snow, *kanko*,
　Jam buns in the meadow are *po po po*.
Taemon, drunk and staggering about,
　Last year ate thirty-eight of them.
Frozen snow, *shinko*, hard snow, *kanko*,
　Buckwheat noodles in the meadow are *ho ho ho*.
Seisaku, drunk and staggering about,
　Last year ate thirteen bowls."

Carried away by the fox's performance, Shinko and Kanko began dancing along with him.

Kikku, kikku, tonton. Kikku, kikku, tonton.
Kikku, *kikku, kikku, kikku, tontonton.*

Shiro sang, "Fox *kon kon*, little fox child. Last year the fox Konbee put his left leg in a snare. Listen to him struggle: *konkon bata-bata konkonkon*."

Kanko sang, "Fox *kon kon*, little fox child. Last year the fox Konsuke found his tail end on fire when he tried to steal a broiled fish. Listen to him cry: *kyan kyan kyan*."

Kikku, kikku, tonton. Kikku, kikku, tonton. Kikku, kikku, kikku, kikkutontonton.

As the three danced along, they gradually entered the forest. The buds of the magnolia tree, so rosy that they seemed to be fashioned of red sealing wax, blew about in the wind, sparkling with light, *pikari pikari*. The indigo shadows of the trees fell like a net covering the forest floor, and wherever the light shown through, it seemed as though silver lilies were in bloom.

By and by the fox, Konzaburo, spoke up. "Shall we invite the deer child also? The fawn is just marvelous at playing the flute."

Shiro and Kanko clapped their hands in delight. Then, they all shouted together. "Hard snow, *kanko*, frozen snow, *shinko*, the fawn wants a bride, wants a bride."

From yonder a soft, pleasant voice called back. "North Wind *whii whii*, West Wind *dohdoh*."

The fox pup Konzaburo looked as though he felt the fawn were making fun of him, and he responded with pouting lips. "That was the fawn. He's so timid that he isn't likely to show up here. But, shall we try shouting again, anyway?"

So the three of them again shouted, "Hard snow, *kanko*, frozen snow, *shinko*, the fawn wants a bride, wants a bride."

Then, from somewhere way off in the distance—whether it was the sound of the wind, or the call of a flute, or the song of the fawn—came this sort of reply.

"North wind *whii whii, kanko kanko*
West wind *doh doh, dokko dokko*."

The fox gave his whisker another twirl and said, "You'll be in trouble if the snow softens, so you'd better be on your way. Please come again when the snow freezes on a moonlit night. We'll show those slides I told you about."

"Hard snow, *kanko*, frozen snow, *shinko*." Shiro and Kanko crossed over the silver snow back toward their home, singing as they went.

"Hard snow, *kanko*, frozen snow, *shinko*."

Part Two: The Magic Lantern Show at the Fox Elementary School

The large bluish-white moon of the fifteenth night rose over Icecap Mountain.

The snow gave off a bluish light, *chika chika*, and today, too, its surface froze as hard as crystallized limestone.

Shiro thought of the promise he had made to the fox, Konzaburo, and spoke softly to his sister, Kanko. "Tonight is the fox's magic lantern show. Shall we go?"

Kanko leaped in the air and shouted, "Let's go. Let's go. Fox *kon kon*, little fox child. *Kon kon*, Konzaburo."

Then, her second-to-oldest brother, Jiro, said, "You're going over to play at the fox's place? I want to go too."

Shiro shrugged his shoulders and said with a troubled look, "But brother, you can't go to the fox's magic lantern show if you're over eleven. It says so right on the tickets."

"What! Show me! Yes, it does say here that with the exception of parents of school pupils, we must politely restrict the attendance of those twelve years of age or older. Those foxes are quite clever. Looks like I can't go. I guess there's no way around it.

Well, if you two are going to go, why don't you take some rice cakes. How about these large, round ones?" Shiro and Kanko put on their tiny snow boots and went out carrying the rice cakes.

Their brothers Ichiro, Jiro, and Saburo stood in a line in the doorway and called out, "Good bye! If you run into an adult fox you're to close your eyes immediately. How about a sendoff? Hard snow, *kanko*, frozen snow, *shinko*, the fox child wants a bride, wants a bride!"

The moon had climbed high up into the sky and the forest was enveloped by bluish-white haze. The two children reached the forest entrance.

There stood a small, white fox pup wearing an acorn badge on its chest. "Good evening. Hurry, please. Do you have your tickets with you?"

"Yes, we do." They pulled them out.

"Over that way, if you please." The fox pup turned its body, and its eyes twinkled as it directed the children with its paw into the depths of the woods.

Moonbeams pierced the forest canopy in diagonal shafts of blue light. The two children reached a clearing. When they looked about they saw that many fox students had already gathered there and were having a lively time hitting each other with chestnut hulls or wrestling with one another. Especially funny was a very, very tiny fox pup, no bigger than a mouse, which was riding on the shoulders of a larger fox pup and trying to catch the stars.

A single white sheet hung from a tree branch in front of them.

Suddenly a voice spoke up from behind, "Good evening. Welcome! I was so pleased to meet you the other day." When the children whirled around in surprise, they saw that it was Konzaburo.

Konzaburo was wearing a splendid swallow-tailed coat with a narcissus blossom pinned to the lapel. He wiped his pointed mouth with a pure white handkerchief.

Shiro gave a small bow and replied, "Please excuse us for inconveniencing you the other day. And thank you very much for tonight. Please share these rice cakes with everyone."

All the fox students looked their way.

Konzaburo threw out his chest and accepted the rice cakes.

"Thank you for going to all the trouble to bring a gift. Please make yourselves comfortable. The slides will begin soon. Do excuse me for a moment."

Konzaburo headed off with the rice cakes.

The little fox students shouted all together, "Hard snow, *kanko*, frozen snow, *shinko*, hard rice cakes are *kattarako*, white rice cakes are *bettarako*."

Next to the curtain appeared a large sign, saying "A donation of many rice cakes has been made by the human Shiro and the human Kanko." The little fox students clapped their paws in delight.

Just then a whistle blew, *whii*.

Clearing his throat, *ehen ehen*, Konzaburo appeared from around the side of the curtain and bowed politely. Everyone grew silent.

"We have beautiful weather tonight. The moon is like a perfectly round plate. The stars look like the sparkling dew on our meadow, now frozen in the sky. Well, the slides are about to begin. I trust that you will look straight ahead at full attention, without blinking your eyes or sneezing.

"Tonight we have two respected guests, so you must all be very quiet. On no condition may you throw chestnut hulls at them. The meeting will now come to order."

Everyone clapped happily. Then Shiro said quietly to Kanko, "Konzaburo certainly speaks well!"

A whistle blew, *whii*.

Large letters appeared on the screen: "One should not drink liquor." Then the letters disappeared, and a photograph took its place. It was a scene of an old man, drunk from too much sake, clutching some strange, round object.

Everyone stamped their feet and sang.

Kikkukikkutontonkikkukikkutonton
"Frozen snow, *shinko*, hard snow, *kanko*,
   Jam buns in the meadow are *po po po*.
Taemon, drunk and staggering about,
   Last year ate thirty-eight of them."
Kikkukikkukikkukikkutontonton

The photograph vanished. Shiro said quietly to Kanko, "That was Konzaburo's song."

Another photograph appeared. A young man drunk from sake had thrust his face in a bowl shaped from a magnolia leaf and was eating something. Konzaburo, dressed in white, was standing at a distance watching this.

Everyone stamped their feet and sang.

Kikkukikkutonton, kikkukikku, tonton
"Frozen snow, *shinko*, hard snow, *kanko*,
    Buckwheat noodles in the meadow are
    ho ho ho.
Seisaku, drunk and staggering about,
    Last year ate thirteen bowls."
Kikku, kikku, kikku, kikku, ton, ton, ton.

The photograph faded away, and a brief intermission began.

A sweet little fox girl brought the two children a tray of millet dumplings.

Shiro suddenly felt weak. After all, he had just seen photographs of bad men like Taemon and Seisaku eating these dumplings, unaware of what they were.

All of the little fox students were looking their way, saying to one another in hushed voices, "I wonder if they'll eat them? I wonder if they'll eat them?" Kanko was so embarrassed that she turned bright red as she sat there holding the plate. Then Shiro made up his mind and said, "Let's eat them. Try some. I really don't believe that Konzaburo would trick us."

The two children ate every single millet dumpling. And how delicious they were! The little fox students were so happy that they jumped up and began dancing.

Kikkukikkutonton, kikkukikkutonton.
"All day long the sun shines, *kankan*,
All night long the moon shines, *shinshin*,
Even if we are made to cry,
The fox students will not tell a lie."

Kikku, kikkutonton, kikkukikkutonton.
"All day long the sun shines, *kankan*,
All night long the moon shines, *shinshin*,
Even if we should fall over and freeze,
The fox students will not be thieves."

Kikkukikkutonton, kikkukikkutonton.
"All day long the sun shines, *kankan*,
All night long the moon shines, *shinshin*,
Even if our bodies are torn asunder,
The fox students will not envy another."
Kikkukikkutonton, kikkukikkutonton.

A whistle blew, *whii*.
Big letters shone across the screen: "Watch
out for traps." Then the letters vanished and
were replaced by a picture. It was a scene of
the fox Konbee with his left foot caught in
a trap. Everyone sang.

"Fox *kon kon*, little fox child, last year the
fox Konbee got his left leg caught in a
trap: *konkonbatabata konkonkon*."

Shiro said quietly to Kanko, "Why, that's
the song I made up!"

When this picture faded out the words "Don't play with fire" appeared. These too faded out and were replaced by a picture. It captured the moment when the fox Konsuke was just about to steal a broiled fish and his tail caught on fire.

All the little fox students shouted.

"Fox *kon kon*, little fox child. Last year the fox Konsuke found his tail end on fire when he tried to steal a broiled fish: *kyan kyan kyan*."

The whistle blew, *whii*, and the screen brightened. Konzaburo came out again and said, "Ladies and gentlemen, this is the end of tonight's show. Something happened tonight that you mustn't forget. Human children, who were not in the least drunk, accepted our food and ate it. So, from now on, even when you become adults, you mustn't tell lies, and you mustn't envy people. If you succeed, you will be able to erase the bad reputation we foxes have earned up until now. This will conclude our meeting."

The fox students were all quite moved. Some waved their hands in the air and others stood up to express their consent. Tears flowed from their eyes.

Konzaburo appeared before the two children, bowed politely, and spoke. "Well, then, good bye. We will not forget the kindness you showed us this evening."

The children bowed good bye and headed toward their home. The fox students ran after them and stuffed the folds and sleeves of their kimono with acorns, chestnuts, sparkling blue stones, and the like. Saying, "Here, these are for you," or "Please take them," they turned around and vanished like the wind.

Konzaburo laughed as he watched them.

The children left the forest and crossed the meadow.

They saw three black shadows heading across the meadow toward them. Their older brothers had come to see them home.

About the Author: Kenji Miyazawa

Kenji Miyazawa is one of Japan's most dearly loved writers. During his brief lifetime he wrote many wonderful stories, poems, and plays. Kenji, as he is fondly known by his first name, was a writer who thought far ahead of his times. Though his work was not well understood while he lived, his ideas are very important to readers today. Japanese children begin reading Kenji's stories in elementary school. As they grow older, they read the stories again and again, enjoying familiar images and discovering new interpretations. Kenji's tales have much to offer readers of all ages.

Kenji was born in 1896 in Iwate Prefecture, about 300 miles north of Tokyo. In his stories we see the landscape of Iwate, ranging from broad plains to densely forested mountains, and from wide rivers to rapid streams cutting through steep valleys. Kenji loved to hike. He knew the names of all the plants near his home, and he could look up at the night sky and tell stories about the constellations. Not everyone in his village had such a good education or so much free time.

When Kenji was a child most of the people in his prefecture made a living by farming. Farmers struggled to survive by growing rice and other crops in a region where winter weather was cold and snowy, and summer rain was unreliable. Hill communities eked out a living making charcoal. Most of Kenji's neighbors were very poor and often had trouble feeding their children. Kenji, on the other hand, came from a wealthy landowning family. His father was a merchant who owned a secondhand clothing store and a pawnshop. When Kenji saw his poor neighbors come to the shop to pawn their few possessions for a little money to buy food, he decided he would devote his life to helping them.

Kenji studied at Morioka College of Agriculture. Later he was able to share his knowledge with local farmers, telling them how to make different kinds of fertilizer and suggesting new varieties of seed they might use. Kenji also taught at an agricultural high school. He was a lively teacher who loved jokes. He did not tell his students what to believe, but rather encouraged his students to have discussions and reach their own opinions. He was a very open-minded man, who had a deep respect for each student's special background and beliefs.

Kenji was a pioneer of environmental education in Japan. He often led his students up the volcanic slopes of Mt. Iwate and took them to a local riverbed to dig for fossils. As they walked, he would tell them about the relationships over space and time between rocks, soil, plants, and animals. He would talk about the water cycle, and the cycle of life and death, emphasizing the interrelationship of all things.

Kenji sought to harmonize Western science with Eastern religion. Kenji's understanding of the interrelatedness of all life and his thoughtfulness toward both the human community and the natural world are founded in his Buddhist beliefs. He felt that we should try to work for the salvation and happiness of all living things, not just for our personal salvation and happiness. We see this message in both his life and his stories.

Kenji died of tuberculosis in 1933 at the age of thirty-seven. A very modest man, unnoticed in his day, he would have been surprised to learn that a museum and research center for the study of his life and writing have been established in his hometown of Hanamaki. Kenji read both English and German, and was well acquainted with children's stories of the West. How pleased he would have been to see his own work read in other cultures.

About the Story: Crossing the Snow (1921)

All over the world there are myths, or ancient stories, that speak of marriage between animals and humans. These stories, like Kenji Miyazawa's *Crossing the Snow*, suggest that people can live as equal members of the natural world in a relationship of trust, understanding, and friendship, rather than in a separate world in which man dominates nature. Kenji shows that this is possible in the innocent world of childhood, but that young people find it difficult to make this special connection once they turn twelve and are drawn toward the world of adults. In crossing the snow, the children are leaving the world of adult human reality, to enter a magical realm in which different kinds of animals can communicate.

Kenji draws us into this magical realm with all of our senses. We see and feel the cold snow. We hear the children's steps as they walk over its surface, and then join the fox in chanting and stamping. We seem to smell the fragrance of white lilies and see their shapes in the snow. Snow and lilies reflect the innocence and purity of childhood. The snow further serves to erase the familiar landscapes of people and animals, placing them on equal footing.

Kenji's story unfolds from the viewpoint of children under twelve. Shiro and Kanko are delighted to be able to cross over the snowy fields on a crisp morning in early spring. The snowy meadows and fields create a bridge between the forest and village. *Crossing the Snow* recalls a children's song from the Tohoku region in which Kenji lived. Children chant the song in early spring as they walk on the crunchy snow, or slide over its slippery surface. During the day the spring sun shines brightly, softening the snow in the rice paddies, vegetable fields, and meadows. When it gets cooler in the evening, these surfaces freeze hard, making them easy to cross. Kenji borrows the song's refrain: *katayuki* (hard snow) *kanko*; *shimiyuki* (frozen snow) *shinko*.

Kenji uses words that imitate the sounds of things

they refer to, drawing us closer to the natural world. In *Crossing the Snow* we can hear the sound of snow crunching under tiny snow boots, *kanko*, and the squeaking of the snow boots over the icy surface, *kikku kikku*. Konzaburo, the fox pup, comes out of the forest, crying *kon kon* and stamping his feet, *kishiri kishiri*. Carried away by the fox's chanting and stamping, the children began to stamp along with him, and the rhythm picks up speed. *Kikku, kikku, tonton. Kikku kikku tonton. Kikku, kikku, kikku, kikkutontonton.*

This children's chant has its origin in a foot-stamping dance that came to Japan from China in the eighth century. In a manner similar to modern American square dance, a caller maintained the rhythm and tempo of the stamping. But, in Japanese tradition, it was thought that as the speed of the stamping and chanting increased, the spirits in the words themselves would leap out, performing a kind of magic spell.

There is magic in the children's words when they call out: "Hard snow, *kanko*, frozen snow, *shinko*. The fox child wants a bride; he wants a bride." Sure enough, a fox appears from the forest. A symbolic wedding takes place between the fox and the little girl as the children enter the forest world of animals. In Japanese folklore the fox is often depicted as cunning or dangerous, and quick to deceive people. Farmers have often looked favorably upon foxes, however, because they catch wild rabbits and mice that devour the crops. Perhaps for this reason, the fox is considered to be the messenger of the god of agriculture. At New Year's, which in the old lunar calendar marked the beginning of spring, farmers offer rice cakes to the god of agriculture; these are the dried rice cakes the brothers send off with Shiro and Kanko as a gift for the foxes.

In Shinto religious belief, a mirror suggests the presence of a god. The children's gifts are mirror-rice cakes, *kagami mochi*, offered before a round mirror. Kenji uses mirror imagery in many ways in this story. A mirror reflects all things, showing their true qualities. Nature mirrors the behavior of our human world.

In *Crossing the Snow*, the basic goodness of the fox is mirrored in the eyes of children. Konzaburo, the fox pup, tells the children about men from their village who drank too much and then ate rabbit pellets, imagining them to be bean-jam buns or bowls of buckwheat noodles. These men claimed to have been bewitched by foxes. But, through Kenji's story, we view the deceptive foxes of folk tales in a new way — through the eyes of the animals and children. The foxes suggest that people are simply deceiving themselves.

In Part II of our story the young children are sent off to the magic lantern show with a warning from their brothers. They mustn't look into the eyes of an adult fox, or they will be bewitched. Konzaburo, on the other hand, who has by now become an adult fox, tells the little fox pups to keep their eyes wide open. The children join the fox pups in watching slides, illuminated by fox fires, and keep their eyes open wide. They share the lessons of the fox children and even dare to eat the dumplings prepared by the foxes.

Early in the story the children cross the snowy meadow and encounter a fox, who they have been told will bewitch and deceive people. At the end of the tale, the children cross the meadow again to return home and encounter three tall, black shadows — the forms of men who snare foxes in traps. For a moment they are afraid, experiencing the same fear that might be felt by the foxes. As they are drawn back to the human world by their brothers, will they retain what they have learned from crossing the snow?

Karen Colligan-Taylor
Fairbanks, Alaska

International Foundation for the Promotion of Languages and Culture (IFLC)
Purpose and Background

With the authorization of the Ministry of Education, Culture, and Science of Japan, the International Foundation for the Promotion of Languages and Culture was established by an endowment from Sunmark Inc. to promote linguistic and cultural exchange throughout the world.

With the 21st century approaching, Japan's role is becoming increasingly important in the realm of cultural and linguistic exchange. It is urgent therefore to encourage and support those who are fluent in more than one language and to promote cultural exchange worldwide. At a time when many nations, both developed and developing, are seeking an interchange of personnel with Japan, we need to take initiatives to aid and promote mutual understanding.

Our mission is to translate and introduce Japanese literature to the world; to translate and introduce to Japan outstanding literature of other countries; to aid and encourage excellent translators of various languages; to provide scholarships to students of all nationalities; to sponsor seminars for language learning; and to conduct translation-proficiency examinations. In these ongoing efforts, our aim is to further linguistic and cultural exchange and mutual understanding throughout the world.

Keiichi Kajikawa, Chairman, IFLC

Translator: Karen Colligan-Taylor

Karen Colligan-Taylor grew up in the suburbs of Tokyo before moving to San Francisco at age ten. She received her B.A. in Japanese Studies at the University of California, Berkeley, and her Ph.D. in Asian Languages and Literatures at Stanford University. As reflected in her Ph.D. thesis "The Emergence of Environmental Literature in Japan" (1986), she has a long-standing interest in the relationship between ecology and literature. Dr. Colligan is currently Professor of Japanese Studies at the University of Alaska, Fairbanks. She has published a number of articles in both Japanese and English on Kenji Miyazawa.

Illustrator: Masao Idou

Masao Idou was born in northeastern China in 1945. After coming to Japan he learned dyeing in Kyoto. He has received many awards as a woodblock artist in Japan. In 1994 he began to illustrate Kenji Miyazawa's world. He has held exhibitions all over the world, including New York, Chicago, Bangkok, and Vancouver.

Crossing the Snow 雪渡り

英語版 宮沢賢治絵童話集 7

2000年3月10日　初版印刷
2000年3月25日　初版発行

協力　　　　　　宮沢賢治記念館、宮沢賢治イーハトーブ館
原作　　　　　　宮沢賢治
翻訳　　　　　　©カレン・コリガン・テーラー 2000
ブックデザイン　鈴木成一デザイン室
本文イラスト　　©井堂雅夫 2000
校正　　　　　　ウィンストン・プリースト
発行所　　　　　（財）国際言語文化振興財団
　　　　　　　　東京都新宿区高田馬場1-32-13 サンマークビル
　　　　　　　　TEL: 03-5273-6660 FAX: 03-5273-6661
発行人　　　　　枻川恵一
発売元　　　　　（株）サンマーク
　　　　　　　　東京都新宿区高田馬場1-32-13 サンマークビル
　　　　　　　　TEL: 03-5272-3166 FAX: 03-5272-3167
印刷所　　　　　大日本印刷株式会社
製本　　　　　　（株）若林製本工場
ISBN4-7631-2317-3 C8390